Do You Love Me More?

Written by Crystal Bowman
and Ava Pennington

Illustrated by Kristi Valiant

Standard® PUBLISHING

Cincinnati, Ohio

Published by Standard Publishing, Cincinnati, Ohio
www.standardpub.com

Text Copyright © 2010 by Crystal Bowman and Ava Pennington
Illustrations Copyright © 2010 by Standard Publishing

Also available: *Will I See You Today?* ISBN 978-0-7847-2917-5, Copyright © 2011 by Standard Publishing.

Printed in: China
Project editor: Elaina Meyers
Illustrator: Kristi Valiant
Cover & interior design: Sandra S. Wimmer

Scripture taken from the *HOLY BIBLE, NEW INTERNATIONAL READER'S VERSION*®. NIrV®. Copyright© 1994, 1996 by Biblica, Inc.™ Used by permission of Zondervan. All rights reserved.

ISBN 978-0-7847-2916-8

Library of Congress Cataloging-in-Publication Data

Bowman, Crystal.
  Do you love me more? / written by Crystal Bowman and Ava Pennington ; illustrated by Kristi Valiant.
      p. cm.
  Includes bibliographical references and index.
  ISBN 978-0-7847-2916-8 (casebound : alk. paper)
  1. Grace (Theology)--Juvenile literature. 2. God (Christianity)--Love--Juvenile literature. I. Pennington, Ava, 1958- II. Valiant, Kristi. III. Title.
  BT761.3.B68 2010
  234--dc22
                              2010036590

16 15 14 13 12 11   1 2 3 4 5 6 7 8 9

From Crystal

To my daughters-in-law, Meghann and Diana. You are gifts of love to our family.

From Ava

To Marilyn Gaeta. You taught me what it means to live a life wholly surrendered to the Lord.

From Kristi

To God, my Heavenly Father, for His unfailing grace and love. And to my dear friends who have encouraged my walk with the Lord, especially Katrina, Cassie, Phil, Joel, Andrea, Alyn, Sarah, Gayla, Tama, Jane, and my Casey. You are precious to me.

I try to do my best each day.
I try to listen and obey.

I try to do the things I should,
so God will see that I am good.

I brush my teeth and comb my hair.
I find my favorite shoes to wear.

My sister likes to play with me.
We chase each other 'round the tree.

We skip and hop, we laugh and sing.
I push my sister in the swing.

My friends come by to have some fun.
I share my toys with everyone.

I eat my carrots and my peas.
I use my manners—I say please.

I help with dishes when we're through.
I even take the trash out too!

I help my mama do the chores.
We wash the dog and sweep the floors.

My mama says, "Come take a look.
I have a very special book.

The Bible is from God above.
It tells us all about his love."

We read the book and then I see,
God sent his only Son for me.

He died for me and took my place.
God's love is free. He calls it grace.

God loves me every single day.
He will not take his love away.

He made me and he loves me so—
all of me from head to toe!

So when I brush my teeth and hair,
and when I'm kind and when I share,

and when I hop and laugh and sing,
and push my sister in the swing,

and every time I eat my peas,
and every time that I say please,

and when I help to do the chores,
like wash the dog and sweep the floors,

I will not wonder anymore,
Do you love me more than you
did before?

I'll do the things that I should do to show you, God, that I love you!

A Note to Parents and Teachers

As you read *Do You Love Me More?* to your children, you may have the opportunity to further clarify the concept of grace as a result of questions or conversation generated by the story.

Grace is the expression of God's love, made freely available to everyone. It's what Jesus Christ did on the cross for us. He owed us nothing, yet gave us everything by restoring our relationship with the Father. Jesus died for our sins so that we do not have to pay the price for our sins.

A common belief in today's society is that good people go to Heaven and bad people go to Hell. This is contrary to what the Bible teaches. The following Bible verses make it clear that no one is good enough to earn salvation:

Romans 3:23, 24 "Everyone has sinned. No one measures up to God's glory. The free gift of God's grace makes all of us right with him. Christ Jesus paid the price to set us free."

Romans 6:23 "When you sin, the pay you get is death. But God gives you the gift of eternal life because of what Christ Jesus our Lord has done."

Ephesians 2:8-10 "God's grace has saved you because of your faith in Christ. Your salvation doesn't come from anything you do. It is God's gift. It is not based on anything you have done. No one can brag about earning it. God made us. He created us to belong to Christ Jesus. Now we can do good things. Long ago God prepared them for us to do."

Isn't God's grace wonderful? The truth is, we cannot do anything to cause God to love us more than he already does. But we can express our gratitude to him by our response. We can receive his free gift of grace and show our gratitude by serving him and others.

In Jeremiah 31:3, God says, "I have loved you with a love that lasts forever. I have kept on loving you with faithful love." That's a great verse to share with your children. Tell your children that God loves them and will keep on loving them—no matter what!

Crystal Bowman is an author, speaker, and Mentor for MOPS (Mothers of Preschoolers). She has written over 60 books for children and three books for women. She also writes stories for Clubhouse Jr. Magazine and lyrics for children's piano music. Her children's books come in all shapes and sizes and many of them have become best sellers. Whether her stories are written in playful rhythm and rhyme, or short sentences for beginning readers, she tries to make them so enjoyable that kids will want to read them over and over again. "But the most important part," she says, "is to teach children that God loves them and cares about them very much." Crystal and her husband live in Florida and have three grown children.

Ava Pennington is an author, speaker, and Bible study teacher. She is the author of *One Year Alone with God: 366 Devotions on the Names of God* (Revell Books, 2010). She also writes for national magazines such as Focus on the Family's Clubhouse, Standard Publishing's The Lookout, and others. Her short stories have appeared in more than twenty anthologies, including fourteen titles in the inspirational Chicken Soup for the Soul book series. Ava has an Adult Bible Study certificate from Moody Bible Institute and teaches a weekly interdenominational Bible study class of more than 200 women. She has a heart for women's ministry, and has been a featured speaker at churches, women's groups, and community events. Ava and her husband live in Florida with their two rescue boxers.

Kristi Valiant is the illustrator of *The Goodbye Cancer Garden*, *Dancing Dreams*, *Oliver's First Christmas*, and *Cora Cooks Pancit* (APALA Picture Book Award winner). She graduated magna cum laude from Columbus College of Art & Design. She lives in Indiana with her husband, her daughter, and a room full of hippos and monkeys. Visit her online at www.kristivaliant.com.